Magic Horses— or Not?

A SIROCCO STORY

By Sibley Miller

Illustrated by Tara Larsen Chang and Jo Gershman

Feiwel and Friends

For Susan. —Sibley Miller

For baby Charlotte—our newest family member and newest
beginning. —Tara Larsen Chang

For Kandis R. Horton, an insightful, encouraging teacher
and a superb equestrian. —Jo Gershman

A FEIWEL AND FRIENDS BOOK
An Imprint of Macmillan

WIND DANCERS: MAGIC HORSES–OR NOT? Copyright © 2011
by Reeves International, Inc. All rights reserved. Distributed in Canada
by H.B. Fenn and Company, Ltd. BREYER,
WIND DANCERS, and BREYER logos are trademarks and/or registered
trademarks of Reeves International, Inc. Printed in February 2011 in China
by Leo Paper, Heshan City, Guangdong Province.
For information, address Feiwel and Friends,
175 Fifth Avenue, New York, N.Y. 10010.

Library of Congress Cataloging-in-Publication Data

Miller, Sibley.
Magic horses—or not? : a Sirocco story / by Sibley Miller ; illustrated by
Tara Larsen Chang and Jo Gershman.
p. cm. — (Wind Dancers ; #12)
Summary: When the tiny flying horses known as the Wind Dancers
suddenly lose their magic, they try to think of it as an adventure and go
in search of Leanna, to whom they have been invisible.
ISBN: 978-0-312-60545-2 (alk. paper)
[1. Horses—Fiction. 2. Magic—Fiction.] I. Chang, Tara Larsen, ill.
II. Gershman, Jo, ill. III. Title.
PZ7.M63373Hok 2011 [Fic]—dc22 2010037706

Series editor, Susan Bishansky
Designed by Barbara Grzeslo
Feiwel and Friends logo designed by Filomena Tuosto

First Edition: 2011

1 3 5 7 9 10 8 6 4 2

www.feiwelandfriends.com

CONTENTS

Meet the Wind Dancers

One day, a little girl named Leanna blows on a doozy of a dandelion. To her delight and surprise, four tiny horses spring from the puff of the dandelion seeds!

Four tiny horses with shiny manes and shimmery wings. Four magical horses who can fly!

Dancing on the wind, surrounded by magic halos, they are the Wind Dancers.

The leader of the quartet is **Kona**. She has a violet-black coat and vivid purple mane, and she flies inside a halo of magical flowers.

Brisa is as pretty as a tropical sunset with her coral-pink color and blonde mane and tail. Magical jewels make up Brisa's halo, and she likes to admire her gems (and herself) every time she looks in a mirror.

Sumatra is silvery blue with sea-green wings. Much like the ocean, she can shift from calm to stormy in a hurry! Her magical halo is made up of ribbons, which flutter and dance as she flies.

The fourth Wind Dancer is—surprise!—a colt. His name is Sirocco. He's a fiery gold, and he likes to go-go-go. Everywhere he goes, his magical halo of butterflies goes, too.

The tiny flying horses live together in the dandelion meadow in a lovely house carved out of the trunk of an apple tree. Every day, Leanna wishes she'll see the magical little horses again. (She's sure they're nearby, but she doesn't know they're invisible to people.) And the Wind Dancers get ready for their next adventure.

CHAPTER 1

A Big (Horse) Surprise

One bright morning, Kona, Sumatra, and Brisa clip-clopped into the kitchen of their apple tree house.

"Where's Sirocco?" Brisa asked between yawns. The jewels in her magic halo were just starting to glimmer in the morning light.

Kona glanced around the kitchen. Next to a nearly empty basket of apple muffins, she saw a scattering of crumbs.

"Clearly, this is one of Sirocco's early-to-rise days," she said dryly. "You know, when he wakes up *way* before we do?"

"And eats way too much breakfast," Sumatra added, "forgets to clean up, and *then* goes out to do show-offy loop-de-loops for all the other early risers in the meadow?"

"Yup!" Kona replied with a laugh.

"That's our *Sirocco*!" Brisa added with a giggle. "Never a serious moment!"

No sooner had the words left her mouth than the colt himself flew through the window. But instead of fluttering cheerily, his wings moved with urgency and he landed with a heavy *clunk*!

"Whoa, horsey!" Kona reprimanded him.

"I'll say," Sumatra added. She pointed with her nose at the muffin basket. "You're liable to knock over the few breakfast muffins you didn't eat yet and leave even more crumbs than you did before!"

Normally, Sirocco would have responded with a "Har, har, har." But this morning? He only scowled, while the magic butterflies in his surrounding halo frowned.

"It's happened!" Sirocco neighed

The fillies blinked at him in confusion.

"*What's* happened?" Sumatra demanded.

"Come with me and see," Sirocco said gloomily. Without another word, he flew back out the window.

Brisa gaped at the other fillies.

"He didn't even pause to gobble another two muffins," she said.

"I *know*," Kona replied, her dark eyes going darker. "This *is* serious. Let's go!"

The anxious fillies flew behind Sirocco as he zinged across the dandelion meadow in a joyless line. No playful pirouettes. No skillful somersaults.

He led them to Leanna's farm.

"Oh no!" Brisa whinnied. "Is something wrong with Leanna?"

Sirocco didn't answer. He didn't stop at Leanna's yellow farmhouse, either. He flew beyond it to the big red barn, the double doors of which were wide open.

As the horses approached the hay-scented barn, they heard a couple of familiar sounds.

The first was Leanna's voice—happy and lilting, as she chattered away.

The second sound was a nicker—the deep, rumbling whinny of a big horse!

"But . . . Leanna doesn't *have* a horse," Sumatra said, confused.

Sirocco turned to her, his eyes stormy.

"*She does now!*" he said.

Once inside the barn, the fillies stopped in mid-air and stared.

Standing in front of a newly built stall strewn with fresh, sweet hay were Leanna and—a pony!

Leanna was smoothing the cute pony's caramel-colored coat with a currycomb.

She was offering him sugar lumps from her pocket.

She was hugging the squat but graceful horse around the neck and kissing his velvety white nose.

"Fillies," Sirocco said, unhappily, "meet Sassy, Leanna's new pet!"

CHAPTER 2
In Sassy's Shadow

After watching Leanna dote on her brand-new pony, the Wind Dancers flew back to their apple tree house to talk.

The ribbons in Sumatra's magic halo sagged.

Brisa's bouncy tail drooped and her magic jewels didn't sparkle.

Kona's magic flowers lost petals.

And Sirocco's head hung.

"How can this be?" Sumatra asked in hurt confusion. "*We're* Leanna's horses!"

"Yes, but she can't see us," Sirocco

reminded her. "Which means she can't pet us or feed us or brush our coats."

"And even if she *could* groom us," Kona added sadly, "we're too little for Leanna to ride."

"Did you see the shiny new saddle in Sassy's stall?" Brisa asked glumly. "It's so pretty. I bet Leanna's going to take her pony out for rides every day."

"That should be us!" Sumatra wailed. "*We* should be Leanna's pets!"

"We *could* have been," Sirocco complained, "if only we weren't magic!"

"Weren't magic?" Brisa asked. "What do you mean, Sirocco?"

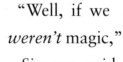

"Well, if we *weren't* magic," Sirocco said, "Leanna would be able to see us and pet us."

"I never thought of that!" Kona said.

Sirocco's eyes went dreamy.

"If we weren't magic," he went on, "Leanna would love us the way she loves her pony—even if we *are* too little to ride!"

The Wind Dancers fell silent—save for some sad sniffles. But before they could get too mopey, Kona spoke up.

"Well, it won't do us any good to sulk," she said. "We can't *wish* Sassy away. And we can't wish our magic away, either! So we'd better get used to it."

"How?" Brisa asked.

"We need to go have an adventure!" Sirocco declared. "It will take our minds off Sassy. It will take our minds off our magic. It will make us *happy*!"

But he didn't sound very happy as he said it.

"We'll need the best adventure *ever* to take our minds off Leanna's new horse!" Sumatra added.

Hoisting himself to his feet, Sirocco plodded over to the tree house's door.

"Let's get to it, then," he said with a sigh.

Without much enthusiasm, he unfurled his wings, preparing to fly over the meadow.

But then something strange happened.

Or rather, *didn't* happen.

Instead of lifting effortlessly into the air, Sirocco's hooves stayed planted firmly on the tree house's wooden floor.

When Sirocco looked down at his heavy feet in disbelief, he noticed something else.

The magical halo of butterflies that fluttered around him day and night had . . . disappeared!

Before Sirocco had the chance to say, "What happened?" Brisa let out a shrill neigh.

"My jewels!" she cried. "My beautiful halo of jewels! It's gone!"

Sumatra, meanwhile, was trying to jump into the air.

"I can't fly!" she neighed. "I'm as heavy as a horseshoe!"

Kona, too, was stunned to find that her flower halo and ability to fly had evaporated like the dew on the dandelions outside.

She blinked with wide, frightened eyes.

"Our magic," she whinnied. "All of our magic is just . . . gone!"

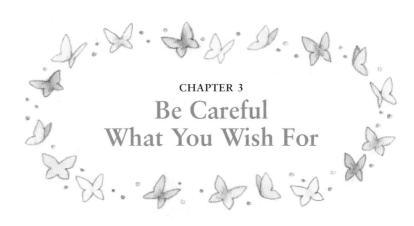

CHAPTER 3

Be Careful
What You Wish For

"How did this *happen*?" Sirocco neighed, rearing up on his hind legs.

"I can't imagine!" Brisa cried, two fat tears squeezing out of her eyes.

Sumatra stared at Sirocco and said, "*I* can imagine!"

"Why are you glaring at me?" the colt demanded with a stomp of his hoof.

"Because," Sumatra replied through gritted teeth, "wasn't it *you*, Sirocco, who said, 'If we weren't magic, Leanna would love us the way she loves her pony'?"

Sirocco's mouth dropped open in shock.

Brisa gasped.

And Kona put on her most mom-like frown of disapproval.

"Sirocco!" she scolded. "You *wished* our magic away!"

"Noooooo!" Sirocco neighed.

"Yesssss!" Brisa and Sumatra neighed back.

"Okay," Sirocco admitted unhappily. "Apparently, I *did* wish our magic away. But how was I supposed to know that would happen?"

"Just wish it back," Kona ordered the colt nervously.

"Good idea," Sumatra echoed. "I've got ribbons to tie, places to fly to."

"Fine," Sirocco said. "I'll wish our magic back. I don't know *how* I'm going to do it, but I guess I'll figure it ou—"

Suddenly, Sirocco bit back his words.

"Well?" Sumatra said impatiently.

"Wait!" Sirocco replied. "I just realized something. I *meant* what I said before! Maybe Leanna *would* love us if she could see us. And now that we're no longer magic, maybe that's possible! Maybe we're not invisible to humans anymore."

"Do you really think so?" Brisa breathed.

"There's one way to find out," Sirocco said. "We have to go see Leanna!"

Kona couldn't help but feel a zing of excitement at the idea of Leanna finally being able to see the Wind Dancers. She could tell by their hopeful faces that Sumatra and Brisa felt the same way.

So she gave Sirocco a firm nod and declared, "Okay. Let's go see Leanna."

"*Awesome!*" Sirocco declared. "I *said* we needed an adventure to take our minds off of Leanna's new pony. And what's more adventurous than making our way in the world as 'regular' horses? I bet I'll be *great* at it. I mean, if Thelma and Benny can do it . . ."

Sirocco snorted as he poked fun at the Wind Dancers' big horse friends, who lived in a paddock at the edge of the dandelion meadow.

"Hmmm," Sumatra grumbled. "Sounds like a *mis*adventure to me!"

"Either way, we don't have a choice," Kona said sensibly. "We'll go right after an early lunch. After all, Sirocco, you're the only one of us who had breakfast!"

"Whoa there," Sirocco said to the violet-black filly, stopping her before she could reach the kitchen. "*Making* lunch? In a *kitchen*? That's not very 'regular' horse, is it?"

"But it *is* very Sirocco," Kona replied. "Do you mean to tell me that you don't want a nice home-cooked meal?"

Sirocco squirmed.

And his stomach growled.

But then he thought about everything that had happened that morning. About seeing Leanna loving her new pony.

About the accusing eyes of the fillies when they'd realized he'd wished away their magic.

About the adventure of living life on the hoof, just like a big horse.

And Sirocco gritted his teeth and nodded firmly.

"That's right. I don't . . . want . . . a home-cooked lunch," he said with some effort.

"What *will* we have for lunch then?" Brisa asked with wide eyes.

"We'll do as the regular horses do!" Sirocco said. He gulped and added, "Graze."

"Graze?" Sumatra said. "On *grass*?"

"No," Sirocco said. "On a succulent salad of alfalfa, clover, *and* . . . grass. Delicious!"

Kona snorted.

"Sirocco smacking his lips over grazing," she said with a laugh. "*This* I've got to see. Okay, let's go!"

Kona began to clop over to the front door before skidding to a halt.

"Oh!" she neighed. "For a minute, I forgot we couldn't fly!"

"And I have no ribbons to make a ladder with," Sumatra complained.

Sirocco gasped, then trotted over to the

door and poked his nose through it.

"How are we going to get down?" he neighed. "We're tree house shut-ins!"

Suddenly, a voice rumbled up from below.

"Maybe you just need to try a little harder, horsey!"

Sirocco peered through the red-gold leaves of the apple tree to find the source of the voice. He felt his heart leap when he spotted a roly-poly squirrel ambling through the grass.

"Gray!" Sirocco called. "My buddy! Make that my best friend in the world!"

Gray gave the colt a wry look.

"'Best friend in the world,' eh?" he said with a laugh. "Tell me, Sirocco—what kind of trouble do you need good old Gray to get you out of this time?"

"Wellllll," Sirocco said sheepishly, "our magic seems to have—"

"—disappeared!" Sumatra finished, giving

the colt a mighty glare. "Thanks to our friend Sirocco, here!"

"Wind Dancers without wind?" Gray mused. "That's like a squirrel with no scamper."

The fuzzy squirrel shuddered at the idea of it.

"I *know*!" Sumatra agreed. "It's terrible!"

"Nasty!" Brisa chimed in.

"Very inconvenient," Kona grumbled.

"*Hello!*" Sirocco jumped in to say. "Have you forgotten about the Leanna factor? About our friend *finally* getting to set eyes on us?"

And love us way more than she could ever adore that pony, he thought to himself.

And that's when Gray hopped onto the apple tree trunk, scampered up to the horses' door, then crouched on their living room floor.

"Anyone care for a ride? Who's first?"

"Gray!" Brisa whinnied with a giggle. "You really *are* our best friend in the world!"

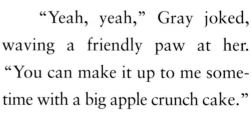 "Yeah, yeah," Gray joked, waving a friendly paw at her. "You can make it up to me sometime with a big apple crunch cake."

And with Brisa clutching the scruff of the
squirrel's neck with her teeth (and uttering
muffled shrieks the entire way), Gray shuttled
the filly to the ground. Three more runs up
and down the tree, and all the Wind Dancers
had landed!

CHAPTER 4

A Day in the Life of a (Non-Magical) Horse

"Our tree house tree sure looks *tall* from all the way down here," Kona said. "And so far away!"

"Which makes our adventure that much more exciting!" Sirocco brayed. "Last one at lunch is a rotten apple!"

Before the fillies could say another word, Sirocco ducked into the tall grass of the dandelion meadow.

"Well," Kona said with a toss of her violet-black head, "all the excitement *has* made me hungry!"

"And a fresh, green salad *would* be pretty," Brisa admitted.

So the fillies trotted into the meadow and followed the sounds of munching to Sirocco. They found him with his mouth too full of grass to talk.

"Ew, this is bitter!" Brisa said, as she nibbled a dandelion leaf.

"Mine's kind of drippy!" Sumatra said, curling her lip at the milky dandelion stem she'd just picked.

Kona pulled up her grass a little too hard and got a dirt-covered root.

"Oh, my!" she neighed. "I guess we're just not used to food that big, ground-bound horses eat."

"What are you talking about?" Sirocco demanded, leaves *still* hanging out of his mouth. "I think this lunch is awesome!"

Then he waited until the fillies looked away before quietly spitting out his wad of grass behind a thicket of dandelions.

Who knew green salads were so . . . earthy! Sirocco thought, trying hard not to cough. After all, he still wanted the fillies to have fun on this adventure. If they did, maybe he would feel a bit less responsible for turning them into non-magical horses.

So—even though his stomach was still rumbling—Sirocco announced, "Whew! I'm stuffed. Are you guys ready to head to Leanna's?"

"Definitely!" Sumatra said. "If Leanna can see us, not only will she love us—hopefully she'll also feed us some better food than this grass!"

"Let's go!" Sirocco whinnied. He pointed his nose in the direction of Leanna's farm and began to canter through the dandelions. His friends trotted alongside him.

"You know, when you fly all the time," Kona said between clip-clops, "you don't realize how much fun it can be to just *run*."

"I *know*!" Brisa said. "I love the way my mane and tail are bouncing in the breeze. Up in the air, I'm prone to terrible tangling!"

"Yeah," Sirocco agreed. "This is the li-*mmmph*!"

The cantering colt was cut off by a giant dandelion puff, which hit him squarely in the face! He skidded to a stop so he could cough and sneeze the fluffy parachutes out of his mouth.

"Yuck!" he whinnied. "That's even worse than the green sal—"

Sirocco caught himself before he admitted how little he'd liked their lunch. Then he threw his golden head back and nickered, "Onward!"

But the Wind Dancers hadn't gotten much further when Brisa stopped in her tracks.

"Oh no!" she cried. "Look!"

Her friends followed her gaze down to her forelegs. Her white socks were mottled with mud and her normally lovely hooves were caked with dirt and grass.

"This is *much* uglier than a few horsehair tangles!" Brisa wailed.

"Leanna will fix it!" Sirocco said quickly. "I bet when she sees you, she'll give you a warm bath. With . . . with flower petals floating in it!"

"I wish I had *flowers* still surrounding me," Kona grumbled, glancing at the empty air around her. She missed the constant companionship of her magic flower halo.

Still, the Wind Dancers pressed on. But now, their canter had slowed to a walk.

"Is it just me," Sumatra piped up, "or is it taking *forever* to get there?"

"We're *so* much faster in flight," Brisa agreed. "Cleaner and prettier, too."

"Now horses," Kona admonished them, "the patient pony gets the prize."

"Wow, that saying is lamer than a lame

horse," Sumatra joked. But mid-giggle, she suddenly lurched forward with a whinny of pain.

"*Owwwww!*" she neighed. "I tripped on a pebble!"

"Talk about a lame horse!" Brisa cried. "Are you okay?"

"I guess so," Sumatra moaned, hobbling a bit on her hurt hoof.

"My hooves are sore, too," Kona said. "All this pounding on the ground—I'm not used to it!"

"Oh, *please*," Sirocco scoffed. "You fillies sure are a bunch of lightweights!"

"We *were*, actually," Sumatra snapped, "back when we could *fly*. It was a *good* thing!"

Sirocco searched his mind for a snappy comeback. But the fact was, his hooves were aching, too.

And his belly felt empty.

And his nose was getting scratched up from pushing through all the plants of the meadow.

And Leanna's farm was still so very far away.

But just when Sirocco felt like he might sit down in the dirt and give up, he spotted something over his head.

It was a split-rail fence.

And not just any fence—it was the fence that enclosed the paddock where Thelma, Benny, Fluff, and Andy lived!

Instantly, Sirocco's energy flooded back. Whinnying with delight, he began cantering toward the fence.

"What are you doing?" Sumatra demanded.

She pointed with her white-striped nose to the right of the paddock. "Leanna's house is *that* way."

"But, clearly, *we* horses need a rest stop," Sirocco said. "And what do you know—here we are at the big horses' paddock!"

"Oh!" Sumatra said. "From *all* the way down here, I didn't even realize!"

Sirocco ignored the sting in Sumatra's comment. Instead, he said, "While we're here, we can show our friends what a great job we're doing at being *regular* horses like them!"

"Well, that *is* cheering!" Kona said with a mischievous gleam in her eyes. The little Wind Dancers and the big horses were lightheartedly competitive about everything from their size to soccer. The little horses were always looking for new ways to best the big.

That's why all the Wind Dancers trotted into the paddock with renewed pride. They tossed their heads and held their tiny tails high.

Still, it took the smallest of the big horses—Thelma's baby colt, Andy—several minutes to even *spot* the Wind Dancers hopping around his hooves. When he did, he let out a long, giggly whinny.

"Okay, Andy," Sirocco said with a frown. "Pipe down. We're not *that* funny!"

Thelma trotted over, gazed down her nose at the Wind Dancers, and whinnied herself.

"I beg to differ," she said. "A Wind Dancer on the ground is *very* funny. And even punier than when you're in the air!"

"Why *aren't* you in the air?" asked Fluff, the sweet filly (and the biggest Wind Dancer fan in the paddock).

"Oh, no reason," Sirocco said, shuffling a front hoof around in the dirt. "You know . . . we . . . just felt like *walking* today."

"No kidding?" replied Benny, who'd trotted up to take his own giggly gander at the grounded Wind Dancers.

"No, Sirocco *is* kidding," Sumatra said. "He *wished* our magic away. So we *can't* fly!"

"Or pop magic jewels, butterflies, ribbons, or flowers out of our halos," Brisa admitted.

"But we're doing *great* at being regular horses!" Kona quickly added, shooting Sumatra and Brisa a scolding look.

"Uh-huh!" Sirocco agreed, grinning big. He trotted in a wide circle around the big horses' hooves to demonstrate. "See? It's *so* easy being you!"

"Now I *know* you're kidding," Thelma said with a snort after watching Sirocco.

"Oh, yeah?" Sirocco asked with a taunt in his voice. "How?"

"Because it took you a full two minutes to run a single circle around us," Thelma said smugly. "Because you're completely out of breath. *And* because all *four* of you are limping!"

"No, we're not," Kona said, jutting out her chin defensively.

"I *love* being ground-bound!" Sumatra declared with bravado.

"Grass tastes *good*!" Sirocco added. But he sounded a *little* less convincing now. (Maybe because he was still out of breath.)

Brisa was the last Wind Dancer to speak up. She *tried* to think of something braggy to say about being a regular horse. But all she could come up with was, "My hooves hurt!"

"Brisa!" Sirocco scolded.

"I'm sorry, but it's true!" Brisa cried. "I miss flying. How do you big horses *do* this every day? Between the dirt and the pebbles and the uneven ground, my feet are in a funk!"

"I knew it!" Benny crowed. "You Wind Dancers are all hot air! You *hate* walking!"

But Fluff was sympathetic.

"We're not stronger than you," she assured Brisa. "It's just that we have shoes that protect our hooves from anything we might stomp on."

"Shoes?!" Brisa said. She gazed at Fluff's glossy, white hooves. She didn't see any laces or buckles.

"Look!" Fluff said, bending her foreleg to lift her hoof off the ground. The Wind Dancers looked at the bottom of Fluff's foot. It was covered by a shiny, U-shaped piece of metal.

"And here I thought horseshoes were just for tossing at a post!" Sumatra said with a laugh. "But you're *wearing* them!"

"And they're *nailed* into your hooves!" Sirocco squeaked, staring at the nail heads dotting the shoe. He felt a little woozy.

"Oh, it doesn't hurt," Fluff was quick to assure the colt. "A horse's hooves are like a person's fingernails. You can't even feel it when you trim them or nail shoes to them—as long as it's done correctly."

"And how *is* it done?" Kona asked.

"By a farrier, of course," Thelma said with a sniff. "A farrier is a blacksmith who levels and trims our hooves, then custom-makes our shoes and nails them on."

"It's like a beauty day!" Brisa breathed.

"Actually, it's your *lucky* day!" Fluff said excitedly.

"Really?" Sumatra asked. "How do you figure?"

"The traveling farrier is here today," Fluff replied. "He drives around the countryside in a big van with all the tools he needs. Then all the horses who live nearby trot over for their shoeing. That's why *my* shoes are so shiny! The farrier just nailed them on this morning!"

"Awesome!" Sirocco said. "Do you think the farrier is still nearby?"

"Oh yes," Fluff said. "It usually takes him all day to get through all the horses who live in our area. His van is parked at our neighbor's barn, just a little ways down the dirt road."

"And *on* the way to Leanna's house!" Sirocco neighed.

"Which is still such a *long* way away," Sumatra grumbled.

"Not to worry!" Sirocco retorted. "With our new horseshoes, getting there will take no time at all!"

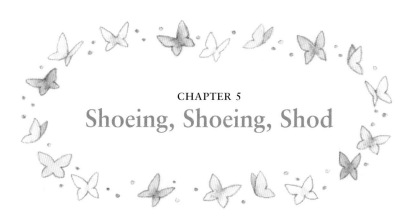

CHAPTER 5

Shoeing, Shoeing, Shod

By the time the Wind Dancers reached the traveling farrier's van, they were hobbling.

They were also arguing.

"I say we just introduce ourselves to the farrier," Brisa proposed. "We're so pretty, he'll be completely enchanted!"

"Or completely shocked!" Sumatra said. "Unlike Leanna, he has *no* idea that we even exist! And you know, adults don't like unfamiliar things."

"Yes," Sirocco agreed, nodding as he limped along the edge of the dirt road.

"Children are much better at believing in magic horses than grown-ups."

"The farrier won't be able to shoe us, anyway," Kona added sensibly. "His hammers and nails are big-horse-sized! So it makes no difference if we introduce ourselves or not. We'll still have to shoe ourselves."

"I just hope we can do it without magic," Sumatra said with a stare.

"Of course we can!" Sirocco blustered. "We may be *magic-less*, but we're still Wind Dancers! We can do anything! Er . . . except fly."

"And beautify things," Kona grumbled, casting a glance at the side of the road. A crushed soft drink can was lying there, tossed by a careless litterer. Normally, Kona would have popped a bunch of magical flowers out of her halo to decorate the can, turning trash into treasure. The fact that she couldn't do so

made her clench her teeth in frustration.

Brisa wasn't happy, either.

"We *also* can't be as pretty as can be," she said. "I bet I look a mess after all this hiking. And I can't even check out my reflection in my mirrored jewels."

"And I just feel *lost* without my ribbons,"

Sumatra noted. "You know how I like things to be tied up neatly in a bow!"

Sirocco fretted as he listened to his filly friends complain. He just *had* to get the Wind Dancers to the yellow farmhouse.

Then we'll be okay, magic or not, Sirocco thought to himself with a desperate grimace. *Because we'll have Leanna!*

Luckily, as the Wind Dancers rounded a bend in the road, Sirocco heard a *clang, clang, clang* of metal hitting metal.

Then he spotted the farrier's van parked in front of a barn.

"We're here!" Sirocco neighed loudly. The horses trotted around the van, then skidded to a halt.

"Wow!" Kona whinnied. "That looks hot!"

The horses ducked behind one of the van's tires and stared at the farrier's furnace. It was part of the horse-shoeing station that the farrier had set up. The roaring fire was mesmerizing.

Just as fascinating was the farrier! He was a burly man in a long, leather apron. With a pair of big tongs, he was holding a glowing, orange horseshoe on an iron block and

pounding at it with a giant hammer. Next he thrust the horseshoe into a bucket of water, where it sizzled. Then he pulled it out and inspected it carefully. Finally, he filed off some rough spots, whistled with satisfaction, and called over to the barn.

"Shoes all ready for Annie!"

A woman emerged from the barn, leading a pretty brown mare by the reins.

"You couldn't have come a moment too soon," the lady told the farrier happily. "Annie is *so* ready for some new shoes!"

"Let's get started then!" the farrier said. He picked up one of the shoes he'd just made and held it up to the big horse's front hoof.

With quick, expert strokes, he used square-headed horseshoe nails to hammer the shoe into the tough outer rim of Annie's hoof. The horse rumbled a bit, but she clearly didn't mind the pounding.

"That is the most awesome thing ever!" Sirocco neighed.

"I *know*!" Sumatra said. "But how are we going to shoe ourselves?"

"We can't get near that fire!" Kona declared. "It's too dangerous."

Sirocco turned to the fillies with a big grin.

"It's not so bad being this close to the ground!" he declared. "It gives you a chance to spot things like . . . this!"

Before the fillies could say a word, Sirocco darted away from the shelter of the van and dashed over to the iron block. He scooped some small, glimmery things from the dirt. Then he cantered over to his friends and spat the glimmery things onto the ground.

"Iron shavings!" Sirocco announced triumphantly. "They're scattered all around the farrier's workspace. They flew off his horseshoes when he was filing them."

"They're the perfect size for our horse-shoes!" Sumatra said with admiration. "But how are we going to get them onto our hooves? We don't have any tiny hammers or nails."

Sirocco frowned at the shavings scattered in the dirt before him. As he gazed at them, he cocked his head to the left. Then the right. Then he walked up to one of the shavings and *stomped* on it with all his strength.

"What are you doing?" Brisa asked.

Sirocco lifted his front hoof and grinned. The iron shaving was stuck to it!

"I noticed that the shavings were all rough and spiky," he neighed. "Each is like a shoe with its nails. Stomp hard enough, and it'll stick!"

"I've got to try this!" Sumatra whinnied. She trotted over to one of the shavings, lifted one of her hooves, and *stomped*.

"*Whoo hoo!*" the filly neighed as she showed off her hoof—perfectly shod—to her friends.

As quickly and as quietly as they could (lest the farrier see and hear them), the Wind Dancers gathered more iron shavings, then stomped all of their feet into their horseshoes. When they finally had sixteen silver feet between them, Sirocco clicked his front hooves together with glee.

Clink!

"Listen to that!" the colt said. "Not only are we shod, we're musical!"

"Ooh!" Brisa said, enchanted. She gave a

little hop, clicking her front hooves together, too.

Clink!

Not to be outdone, Sumatra found a flat rock nearby and began stomping all over it.

Clickety, clackety, click!

"Uh, what are you doing?" Sirocco asked.

"I'm tap dancing, of course!" Sumatra said with a grin. "I've always been the airy dancer of our group. Now, I'm just adapting to life on the ground!"

All of Sumatra's legs seemed to be going in different directions at once.

"Very graceful, Sumatra," Kona said with a smile.

"Thank you!" Sumatra neighed, before tripping over her hooves and sprawling in the dirt.

The tap-dancing Wind Dancer lifted her head woozily.

"I guess what I was getting ready to say," she whimpered, "is thank you . . . for helping me up after I fall on my face!"

"Ohhhh," Brisa cried sympathetically as she rushed to help Sumatra up. "And just look at the unsightly dirt you have all over your pretty silvery blue coat now!"

"Well," Sumatra sighed as Brisa brushed her off with her tail, "tapping on the ground is certainly *different* from dancing in the air!"

"And different is good!" Sirocco rushed to say. "Different is *adventurous*!"

"Speaking of that," Kona pointed out, "now that our hooves are protected from the ground, we can get on with *our* adventure!"

"Right!" Sirocco neighed. "If we take the shortcut, it's only another mile or so until we see Leanna. And, more importantly, until she sees us!"

"A mile!" Brisa cried. "That's nothing!"

"From the air," Sumatra reminded her. "On the ground? Who knows how long that will take."

Brisa's face fell.

"By the time we get there, I'll be utterly unbeautiful!" Brisa cried. "I don't want *that*

to be Leanna's first glimpse of me!"

"Face it!" Sumatra snapped. "Without our

pretty halos, we're *all* looking a little plain."

"A Wind Dancer without a halo," Kona agreed primly, "is like a pinto without its 'paint.'"

"A show horse without a show ring," Brisa added.

"A cow horse without . . . well, cows!" Sumatra chimed in.

"Forget what we've lost and think about what we're about to gain," Sirocco whinnied. "Leanna! Unless, of course, we never get there because you fillies are too busy complaining!"

Sirocco's friends couldn't argue with that. So instead, they cheered up, and once more headed toward Leanna's pretty, yellow farmhouse.

CHAPTER 6

Leanna, at Last

The Wind Dancers cantered through the dandelion meadow, enjoying the sturdy feel of their horseshoes and the rustle of soft grass. The sun kept them warm.

"You know," Sirocco said, as he traveled alongside his friends, "it was a day much like this one that Leanna blew us out of our dandelion!"

"You're right!" Sumatra said. "And that was the first—not to mention the last—time that Leanna ever saw us."

"And only for a fleeting moment, at that,"

Kona reminded her. "Then we disappeared into our magic halos, right before her eyes."

"Which is why she's going to be that much more excited when she sees us again!" Sirocco said. His canter quickened to a gallop at the thought.

The fillies were excited, too—so much so that they were finally able to put aside their yearning for their magic.

"I don't think I need my jewels to help me with my grooming after all," Brisa pointed

out. "This soft grass is combing out my mane and tail as we run through it. It's almost as handy as magic!"

Sumatra paused to pluck a long, emerald blade of the grass and tie it into a pretty bow.

"I'm doing pretty well without my ribbons, too," she said.

"And *I* have plenty of flowers to brighten my day," Kona said as she spotted some vivid, violet morning glories, twined around a nearby fencepost.

"Sirocco!" Kona added with a twinkly smile. "Look what *else* I see over there!"

Sirocco slowed down and glanced at the flowers without much interest—until he saw what Kona was referring to. Then he skidded to a halt.

Swarming all around the flowers were . . . butterflies! All of them of different colors.

Sirocco stared at them. He was accustomed to flying around in a magic halo of the flittering insects, morning, noon, and night. But he hadn't realized until just this moment how strange it had been spending the day without his little magical friends.

Only when these real butterflies had gotten their fill of nectar and flown away did Sirocco resume his journey toward Leanna's house.

"Now, didn't that make you happy," Brisa chirped as she trotted next to Sirocco, "to spot some butterflies like your old ones?"

Sirocco just nodded. He didn't want to admit that the real butterflies had made him *un*happy. After all, it was his fault that *his* butterflies had gone away, along with Brisa's jewels, Sumatra's ribbons, and Kona's flowers.

He also didn't want to dampen his friends' happy moods.

Little did he know, something else was going to do that for him—just then.

"Ew!" Brisa said as the grass began to thin. "The dirt here is wet and sticky. My new horseshoes are going to get dirty!"

A few steps more and the ground got wetter still.

"Oh, no!" Brisa cried, slowing to a tiptoe.

After walking another few yards, the Wind

Dancers realized why they were feeling stuck in the mud. They'd arrived at a burbling stream with a wet, mucky bank.

"Hey!" Sirocco said in surprise. "How come we've never seen this brook before?"

"I guess because we were always flying so high *above* it," Kona replied. "At top speed, I might add!"

"I'm sure I've noticed it," Sumatra added. "But it must have looked so small from up in the sky, I never gave it a thought!"

The Wind Dancers stared at the stream.

"It sure doesn't look like a trickle now," Brisa said in a small voice.

The water flowed swiftly, making bubbling noises as it went.

The horses peered to the left and then to

the right. The stream had no end in sight.

"We can't walk across," Kona said, thinking hard. "It's too wide and too deep."

"If I had my ribbons, I could weave us up a rope bridge," Sumatra offered. "But I don't think a grass bridge would hold us."

"If I had my jewels," Brisa added, "I could have made them into stepping stones."

"Maybe we could try floating across," Sirocco piped up. "We could spread out our wings like sails on boats!"

"That could work," Kona said skeptically. "*Or* our wings could get waterlogged and heavy, dragging us under the current." Then she added: "We know how to swim a little bit, but this looks like too much."

Sirocco tried to come up with another option, or at least, a dose of cheer. But after searching for cheery ideas all day long, he was clean out of them!

Instead, he neighed, "Now what?" and stamped his hoof in the mud.

"Sirocco!" Brisa squealed. "You splashed mud on my beautiful coat! Leanna—"

"—won't ever see your beautiful coat," Sirocco said. "So it doesn't matter anyway."

"What do you mean by that?!" Sumatra demanded.

"We're stuck!" Sirocco said. "We got down from our tree house without magic today. We made ourselves horseshoes without magic. We even managed to be *happy* without magic. At least, for a little while."

The fillies exchanged troubled glances.

"But *this*," Sirocco said, pointing with his nose at the deep stream, "has us stumped!"

"Stymied," Kona agreed with a sorrowful shake of her head.

"Stopped," Sumatra added, hanging her head.

"And we were so close to Leanna's farm!" Brisa wailed in disappointment.

"Who knows if it would have helped anyway," Sirocco said sadly. "Even if Leanna can see us now, we just can't compete with her pony."

"Right," Sumatra replied. "We already know a girl wants to be able to ride her horse!"

"And grooming a Wind Dancer would take her only about thirty seconds—*bo-ring*!" Brisa added.

"And all she'd have to put in our trough is a few oats," Kona noted unhappily. "Which isn't exactly thrilling for a pet owner."

"I don't know why I even *thought* we should try this adventure," Sirocco pouted. "I wish we could just go back to our old life.

I miss our house. I miss being in the air. I miss my butterflies. I miss—"

"—the Wind Dancers."

Sirocco jumped. His rant was interrupted by a girl's chirpy voice.

By *Leanna's* chirpy voice talking about the Wind Dancers! Over the tall grass on the other side of the stream, the little horses couldn't see Leanna yet. But they could hear her, along with the rhythmic breaths and *tromp-tromp-tromp*ing hooves of her pony walking through the grass.

"Oh, you'd just *love* them, Sassy!" Leanna was telling her pony. "They were the prettiest, most amazing horses I ever saw, even if I only saw them for an instant, just once."

Sassy nickered, as if in reply. The Wind Dancers heard Leanna pat the big horse with a warm *thumpity-thump-thump*.

Then Leanna went on to talk about that day—the Wind Dancers' first day—with her voice full of wonder.

"It was a day a lot like this one, actually," Leanna said. The Wind Dancers looked at each other with bright eyes. They'd just been saying the same thing! "I blew on a big dandelion and out popped four horses! Beautiful flying horses, colorful tiny horses, horses with shimmering wings. They had halos too. Of butterflies, flowers, jewels, and ribbons. I couldn't believe it. But they disappeared as quickly as they'd come."

Now the light in the Wind Dancers' eyes dimmed.

"Maybe," Sumatra said, "now that she has a 'real' horse, Leanna doesn't really believe in us anymore."

Before Sirocco could reply, Leanna and her pony came into view. Leanna's cheeks were pink and her hair was tousled from riding. Sassy ambled down to the stream and stepped over it effortlessly. The rushing brook that had thwarted the Wind Dancers was nothing but a little speed bump to the life-sized pony.

"The strange thing is," Leanna confided to her horse as they walked closer to the Wind Dancers, "I know my little Wind Dancers are still out there. Somewhere."

Leanna looked around the pretty meadow with a smile and a sigh.

"Sometimes they leave little presents for me," Leanna said. "Like they're watching over me, always nearby."

Sassy rumbled, again sounding as if he were chatting. Leanna seemed to think so, too, because she laughed.

"It's nice to be able to tell someone about the Wind Dancers," she said with a smile. "Nobody else would believe me!"

Then she added: "I *know* they're real. Even if I never see them again!"

Sirocco was so excited, he reared back on his hind legs, kicked the air, and whinnied.

"I've never been so happy to be wrong!" he neighed. "Leanna loves us! Even if she can't see us! She loves us just as much as Sassy."

The fillies joined in on Sirocco's happy celebration, whinnying and kicking their horseshoed hooves. It was only after they finished their dance of joy, breathing hard, that Kona cocked her head.

"It's kind of funny, isn't it?" she asked.

"Now that Leanna can see us, we realize that she doesn't *need* to see us."

Sirocco gasped and stared at the violet filly.

"I'd almost forgotten!" he whinnied. "Leanna *can* see us now!"

The Wind Dancers looked at each for one electric moment. Then they came to a wordless agreement. Whether or not Leanna *needed* to see the Wind Dancers to love them completely, it would *still* be a thrill to finally come face-to-face with her.

To watch her light up with joy when she saw them.

To feel her fingertips petting their heads and stroking their noses.

To hear her talking to *them* the way she chatted with her pony.

Together, the Wind Dancers launched themselves into the air and darted over to their friend. They hovered before Leanna's pretty face and waited for it to light up with recognition and joy.

But . . . nothing happened!

Leanna looked straight through the Wind Dancers, as if she didn't see them at all.

And that's when Sirocco gasped again and realized *the Wind Dancers had just launched themselves into the air!*

"We're . . . we're flying again!" Sirocco squeaked.

Brisa whinnied!

Sumatra neighed!

Kona tossed her head and twirled in the air.

"I was so excited to see Leanna, I didn't even realize it!" the violet horse gasped.

"None of us did!" Sirocco neighed.

As he spoke, Sirocco realized that Kona's halo of beautiful, bouncing flowers had returned.

Brisa's jewels were back, too, as

sparkly as ever! Sumatra's blue, green, and purple ribbons flowed around her again, too, as prettily as the little stream flowed through the meadow.

Finally, Sirocco glanced around himself and saw his old pals, the butterflies, flittering and fluttering a happy hello.

"I can't believe it!" Sirocco said. "I must have wished our magic back! I didn't even know I was doing it!"

The Wind Dancers hovered in the air and watched Leanna and Sassy continue across the meadow—away from them.

"She never even knew we were here!"

Kona said with wonder in her voice.

"Except," Sirocco reminded her, "she kind of did! Like Leanna said, she's always known we were nearby. She's *always* loved us!"

"Still," Brisa said with just a hint of a pout, "it would have been nice to have gotten our magic back *after* Leanna got a glimpse of us. Even just a little one! We came all this way, after all!"

Kona smiled at Brisa.

"I think it's safe to say that whatever Leanna would have seen of us, she would have liked," she said.

"She likes us just the way we are!" Sumatra added, doing a happy flip in the air.

"I wouldn't have it any other way," Sirocco said with a big grin.

And he meant it.

He knew that he'd wish for things again. For more adventures. For new ways to have fun with his friends. For an endless supply of appley treats.

But never again would Sirocco wish to be anything other than what he was—a tiny, magical, flying horse. Invisible to people, but loved just the same.

As they came together in a sweet group nose nuzzle, Sirocco felt sure that Sumatra, Kona, and Brisa felt exactly the same way.

And then—as they did at the end of each adventure—the Wind Dancers headed home. Never before had they flown with this much excitement, this much gratitude, this much joy.

I Think I Hear Them Calling My Name

Trotting along on her pony—far below the once-again flying Wind Dancers—Leanna thought she heard something sweet in the air.

A distant echo of a whinny.

A faint, tinkling neigh.

And maybe, just maybe, deep down, Leanna knew that what she heard was the sound of her happy Wind Dancers. Always nearby, always close to her heart.